Betsey Biggalow

Hurricane Betsey

Also by Malorie Blackman

Betsey Biggalow is Here!
Betsey Biggalow the Detective

MALORIE BLACKMAN

Betsey Biggalow
Hurricane Betsey

Illustrated by Lis Toft

MAMMOTH

To Neil, with love

First published in Great Britain 1993
by Piccadilly Press Ltd
Published 1994 by Mammoth
an imprint of Reed International Books Ltd
Michelin House, 81 Fulham Road, London SW3 6RB
and Auckland, Melbourne, Singapore and Toronto

Reprinted 1995

Text copyright © Malorie Blackman, 1993
Illustrations copyright © Lis Toft, 1993

The right of Malorie Blackman to be identified as author
of this work and of Lis Toft to be identified as illustrator
has been asserted by them in accordance with the
Copyright, Designs and Patents Act 1988

ISBN 0 7497 1423 9

A CIP catalogue record for this title
is available from the British Library

Printed and bound in Great Britain
by Cox & Wyman Ltd, Reading, Berkshire

CONTENTS

Betsey Plays Finders Keepers!   1

Hurricane Betsey!   14

Betsey and the Insult Contest   26

Betsey and the Monster Hamburger 40

Betsey Plays Finders Keepers!

"It's mine! It's mine! I found it! Finders keepers!" said Betsey.

Sherena, Betsey's bigger sister, raised her head from her History homework book.

"What have you found?" asked Sherena.

"This shell necklace. Isn't it pretty?" Betsey replied. She held it up high for her sister to see. "I found it here on my bed."

1

"Betsey, you know very well that necklace is mine," frowned Sherena.

"No I don't." Betsey shook her head. "It hasn't got your name on it and it was on *my* bed. So it's mine! Finders keepers!"

"Betsey, you toad! Give that back," ordered Sherena.

"Won't! Won't! Won't!" said Betsey.

Sherena stood up, her eyes flashing like lightning. "Betsey, I'm warning you. Give that back."

"Gran'ma . . . GRAN'MA!" Betsey yelled. And she ran out into the sitting-room with Sherena chasing after her, trying to snatch back her necklace.

"What on earth is going on?" asked Gran'ma Liz.

"Tell Betsey to give me back my necklace, before I get annoyed," said

2

Sherena crossly.

"It's not her necklace. It was on my bed. It's mine! Finders keepers!" said Betsey.

Gran'ma Liz frowned. "Betsey child! You know as well as I do that that necklace belongs to your sister. Give it back."

"But Gran'ma . . ."

"Elizabeth Ruby Biggalow! Give it back. Don't let me have to tell you again," said Gran'ma Liz.

There was Gran'ma using Betsey's whole, full name! That meant that Betsey had better step carefully or the next step might get her into a lot of TROUBLE!

"Botheration!" Betsey muttered under her breath. Reluctantly, she handed the necklace back to Sherena.

"Hhumph!" said Sherena, before

marching back to her bedroom.

Betsey wandered out into the back yard, muttering to herself all the while.

"I *found* that shell necklace on *my* bed," Betsey said to herself. "So it should've been mine. It didn't have Sherena's name on it . . ."

Then Betsey spied a cricket ball, lying in the middle of the yard. She ran over to it and picked it up.

"I found it! It's mine! Finders keepers!" smiled Betsey.

"What are you mumbling about?" Desmond, Betsey's bigger brother, called out from across the back yard.

"Look what I've found, Desmond," beamed Betsey. And she held up the cricket ball for her brother to see.

Desmond frowned. "You've found my cricket ball there because that's where I put it."

"This cricket ball was lying there, waiting for someone to find it - and that's me!" said Betsey. "This is my cricket ball now."

"Betsey, give me back my ball," said Desmond.

"I won't! It doesn't have your name on it," Betsey replied.

"Betsey, I'm warning you . . ." Desmond said.

"Won't! Won't! Won't!" said Betsey. "This ball is mine."

"Right!" And with that, Desmond started chasing Betsey all around the garden. Betsey ducked around the breadfruit tree and ran through the chickens with Desmond racing after her.

"BETSEY! COME BACK HERE!" Desmond yelled.

Betsey ran into the house, followed by her brother.

"Wait a minute!" said Gran'ma Liz. "If you two want to chase each other then go and do it in the back yard, not in the house."

"Gran'ma Liz! Tell Betsey to give me back my ball," Desmond said.

"It's not his ball. I found it in the back yard," Betsey argued.

"Betsey! What has got into you today?" asked Gran'ma Liz. "You know as well as I do that that ball belongs to your brother."

"But . . . "

"No 'buts'!" said Gran'ma Liz. "Give Desmond back his ball."

And although Betsey huffed and puffed and pouted, she had to hand over the cricket ball. Sherena came out of her bedroom just as Betsey went out into the back yard.

"What's going on?" Sherena asked.

"Betsey's playing silly games," sniffed Desmond. "She took my cricket ball and insisted it was hers just because I wasn't holding it at the time."

"She did the same thing to me. She said my shell necklace was hers just because I didn't put my name on it," said Sherena.

"I think it's time we taught Betsey Biggalow a lesson," winked Gran'ma Liz.

So Sherena and Desmond

gathered around her as Gran'ma Liz told them of her plan.

That evening, Uncle George came round for dinner. While Betsey was out of the room, Gran'ma Liz grabbed Uncle George for a quick, secret chat. Then they all sat down to dinner - and what a dinner it was too! Vegetable and dumpling soup, the way only Gran'ma Liz and Mam could make it.

"Betsey, what have you been up to today?" asked Uncle George.

Betsey glanced at Sherena who was staring at her. Then Betsey glanced at Desmond who was glaring at her.

"Er . . . nothing much, Uncle George," said Betsey, taking another spoonful of her soup.

"Betsey! What's that behind you?" Sherena suddenly called out.

Betsey quickly turned her head.

"Where? Where?"

"Over there," said Sherena, pointing to the corner of the ceiling.

"I can't see anything," Betsey frowned. Betsey turned back to her soup. The bowl was empty . . . Betsey stared and stared, but it didn't help. Her bowl was still empty.

"Where's my soup gone?" Betsey asked, amazed.

"Oh, was it your soup?" asked Uncle George. "I didn't know that. It was just sitting on the table, so I helped myself."

"But . . . but . . . but that was *my* soup," Betsey spluttered.

"It didn't have your name on it, Betsey," said Gran'ma Liz. "So how was your uncle to know it was yours?"

"Because . . . because . . . the bowl was in front of me," said Betsey.

"But the whole table is in front of me. So the table and everything on it is mine." said Uncle George. "Finders keepers!"

"But that's not fair," said Betsey.

"In fact, not only does the table and everything on it belong to me, but everyone at the table belongs to me too!" said Uncle George.

And Uncle George stood up and went over to Betsey. Before she could say 'dumplings!', Uncle George picked her up and threw her over his shoulder.

"Look what I've found everyone," grinned Uncle George. "This girl was just sitting here and I found her. As she hasn't got anyone's name on her, I'm going to keep her. Finders keepers!"

"You can keep her for as long as you like, Uncle!" said Desmond.

"Uncle! Uncle! Put me down," yelled Betsey.

"Who said that?" said Uncle George, looking around.

"I said it, Uncle George. Put me down," said Betsey.

"Why?"

"Because I . . . I don't belong to

11

you," said Betsey.

"Who do you belong to then?" asked Uncle George.

"I belong to . . . myself," Betsey decided.

"Where does it say that?" asked Uncle George.

"It doesn't say that anywhere. But it's true," said Betsey.

"What about this shell necklace? Whose is it?" asked Sherena, holding up the necklace for Betsey to see.

"It's yours. Mam gave it to you for your last birthday," Betsey replied.

Desmond held up a cricket ball. "And who does this belong to?" he asked.

"It's yours," said Betsey. "It's the special one Dad bought for you."

"So have we heard the last of this finders keepers nonsense?" asked Gran'ma Liz.

"Yes! Yes! I'm never going to say those two words ever, *ever* again," said Betsey.

"In that case, I'll put you down," said Uncle George. And he put Betsey back on her feet.

"And I'll give you some more soup," smiled Gran'ma Liz.

Gran'ma Liz filled Betsey's bowl with some soup from the pot. Betsey helped herself to some more dumplings.

When Sherena finished her soup, she peered into the pot.

"Gran'ma Liz, are there any more dumplings left?" asked Sherena.

"Sorry, Sherena. Betsey had the last one," Gran'ma Liz replied.

"Finders keepers!" said Betsey.

Hurricane Betsey!

"Sherena, Desmond, Betsey, come in here a minute," called Mam.

Sherena came in from the back yard where she was polishing her bike. Desmond came in from his bedroom where he was doing his homework - for once! Betsey was already in the sitting-room.

"What's the matter, Mam?" asked Sherena.

Mam looked very worried.

"I've got some bad news," said Mam at last. "There's just been a hurricane warning on the TV. Hurricane Boris is heading this way."

"A hurricane?" asked Betsey.

"Oh, you've never seen a hurricane, have you?" said Desmond, his eyes big and round like saucers. "A hurricane is like a huge, ferocious storm with winds gusting at over one hundred and fifteen kilometres an hour. The winds are so strong, they can lift you right off your feet and they can blow down trees and blow the roofs off houses and make the sea spin with giant waves and . . ."

"That's quite enough, Desmond," said Mam sternly.

"Will we spin up and up in the air as well?" asked Betsey quickly.

"Of course not," said Mam. "As long as we stay in the house, we'll be fine."

"But I *want* to spin up and up in the air," said Betsey, very disappointed. "I want to fly."

"Then you'll just have to wait until you fly in an aeroplane like the rest of us," said Sherena. "If a hurricane spun you up in the air, when you landed you'd probably break almost every bone in your body . . ."

"That's quite enough from you as well, Sherena," frowned Mam.

"What should we do, Mam?" asked Desmond.

"I want the three of you to help me pack away all the breakable things," said Mam.

Betsey stared and stared.

"What's the matter, Betsey?" asked Mam.

"I don't want to be packed away! I don't want to be packed away!"

Betsey sniffed, very close to tears.

Everyone burst out laughing.

"Betsey, child! We're not going to pack *you* away," said Gran'ma Liz.

"We'd never find a box big enough!" muttered Desmond.

"We're going to pack up my best plates and glasses and anything else that's fragile," Mam told Betsey.

"Fragile?" said Betsey.

"That means easily breakable,"

Sherena told her. "And Betsey, you
aren't fragile!"

So that's what they did. Betsey and
Sherena and Desmond wrapped up
Mam's best glasses and plates and
ornaments in newspaper before
putting them into boxes.

"Mam, where do we go so we don't
get swirled up and whirled up into
the air?" asked Betsey.

"We'll stay in the sitting-room,"
Mam answered.

"Will we be safe?" asked Betsey,
anxiously.

"Of course. We'll be together,
won't we?" smiled Gran'ma Liz.

"Sherena, bring your bike in from
outside, and Betsey, go and get
Prince from the back yard please,"
said Mam.

Prince was the family Alsatian dog.

Betsey ran out into the back yard

to fetch him. Once outside, Betsey noticed that the leaves of the breadfruit tree were jiggling madly, as if dancing to some music that Betsey couldn't hear.

"A hurricane is coming! A hurricane is coming!" Betsey shouted out.

And she whirled and twirled around, knocking the flowerpots off the ledge beside her.

"BETSEY! Bring Prince inside and stop dancing about," said Gran'ma Liz. "Hurricanes are serious business and nothing to be glad about."

"Yes, Gran'ma," said Betsey.

Betsey looked up at the sky. It was dark and grey and she couldn't see the sun. A drop of water landed on her forehead, then another drop landed on her cheek. The storm was beginning. Betsey called Prince over

and together they went into the
house.

"What else should I do, Mam?"
asked Betsey.

"Now we have to board up all the
windows so that they don't blow in
on us," said Mam, looking around.

"Sherena, Gran'ma and I will do
that. You and Desmond fill all the
flasks in the house with water. Then
make sure that the bath tub and the
sink are clean and fill them with cold

water as well."

"Why do we have to do that?" asked Betsey.

"The hurricane might disrupt the water supply, so we should make sure we've got enough drinking water to last us for a while," Mam explained.

For the rest of the morning, the whole family was busy, busy, busy, but at last everything was done.

"Desmond, bring your homework in here so you can carry on with it," said Gran'ma Liz.

"Do I have to?" Desmond pleaded.

"Yes, you do. Sherena, if you've got any homework, you might as well do it now too," said Gran'ma Liz.

"We'll all stay in this one room and watch the TV for news of the hurricane," said Mam.

Betsey sat next to Mam, who put

her arm around Betsey's shoulders.

"Will we be all right?" Betsey whispered.

"Of course we will," smiled Mam.

Outside, Betsey could hear the heavy rain splashing against the roof and the windows and she could hear the wind howling around the house.

"Please stay in your homes and listen to your radios or your TVs for further information. Please do not use your phones unless it is an emergency. Please stay in your homes and listen to your radios or your TVs for further information."

"What's that?" Betsey squeaked.

"Don't worry, Betsey. It's just the police, advising people about what they should do," said Mam. "They'll drive around for as long as they can, talking through a loudspeaker so that everyone can hear them."

"Oh!" said Betsey, and she cuddled up closer to Mam.

A while later, an announcement came on TV.

"This is a hurricane update. The hurricane has changed course and is now heading out to sea. Repeat. The hurricane has changed course and is now heading out to sea."

"Thank goodness for that." Gran'ma Liz gave a sigh of relief.

"We're still going to get stormy weather for a while but at least the hurricane won't be passing this way," said Mam. "Okay, everyone, let's start unpacking the boxes and putting everything back in its place."

Betsey sprang up off the sofa and ran to the nearest box.

"I'll help. Let me help," she said, picking up the box which was filled with a few glasses wrapped in

newspaper. Betsey whirled and
twirled around with the box in her
hands. "The hurricane has gone! The
hurricane has gone!" she grinned.
But because of the box, Betsey didn't
see that she was heading straight for
Prince . . .

"No, Betsey . . ."
"Don't . . ."

Too late. Betsey tripped over Prince and the box of glasses in her hands went flying up into the air to land with an enormous **SMAAAAASH-CRAAAAASH**! All of the glasses in the box were shattered!

Betsey stared at the box.

"Is everyone all right? No one got cut, did they?" asked Mam.

Everyone was fine - except Betsey.

"Mam, it wasn't me. It was . . ." Betsey began.

"Betsey, sit on the sofa and watch the TV," interrupted Gran'ma Liz. "You're causing more damage than the hurricane would've done! In fact I know what we should call you . . ."

And everyone shouted out, "Hurricane Betsey!"

Betsey and the Insult Contest

Betsey came home from school, with her chin drooping and her mouth frowning and tears in her eyes.

"Betsey child, what's the matter with you?" asked Gran'ma Liz, immediately concerned.

"I . . . I had a quarrel with May," Betsey whispered.

"A quarrel? What about?" asked Gran'ma.

Betsey didn't answer. She just shook her head and stared down at her sandals.

That evening, Betsey hardly touched her dinner. It was one of her favourites too - flying fish and french fries and fresh salad. There was a huge jug of orange juice in the middle of the table but Betsey didn't ask for seconds and thirds the way she usually did. She drank half a glass of orange juice and left the rest. Gran'ma Liz and Sherena and Desmond looked at each other, then at Betsey. They were beginning to get worried.

After dinner Betsey moped around the house, sighing and sniffing and not saying a word, until Desmond and Sherena couldn't stand it any more.

"Betsey, what did you and May

have an argument about?" asked
Sherena.

"Nothing much," Betsey replied.

"Go on. You can tell us. Why did
you and May have a bust up?"
Desmond asked.

"I'm not telling you," sniffed
Betsey.

"Come on, Betsey. We want to
help," said Sherena.

"Yeah! I miss having you bouncing
around the house and chatting so
much I can't hear myself think," said
Desmond.

"So why did you and May fall out?"
said Gran'ma Liz.

"It doesn't matter," sighed Betsey.
And off she walked.

At last Mam came home, but
Betsey wouldn't even tell Mam what
was wrong. She just wandered
around the house, her face as long as

a tree trunk, saying, "It doesn't matter. It doesn't matter."

"Mam, do something," Sherena whispered, when Betsey couldn't hear.

"She's driving us nuts!" said Desmond. "I thought Betsey was bad enough when she made a lot of noise, but she's even worse when she's quiet!"

"All right, then," said Mam. "Let me phone up May's mam. Maybe May told her what's going on."

So Mam phoned May's house and was on the phone for quite a while. When at last she put the phone down, Mam had a deep frown on her face.

"Well? What's going on?" asked Gran'ma Liz.

"May won't tell her mam what they quarrelled about either," said Mam.

"I think it's time for me to take the matter into my own hands."

"What d'you mean, Mam?" asked Desmond.

"You'll see." That's all Mam would say.

The next day was a Saturday. A beautiful, sunny Saturday with not a cloud in the sky. Not that Betsey noticed. She moped around the house quieter than a mouse.

"Betsey, do you want to ride my bike?" Sherena asked.

"No, thank you," said Betsey, her head bent.

Sherena stared at her in amazement. Betsey had never before said no to riding Sherena's bike. Usually Betsey pouted and pestered and badgered and bothered Sherena for a ride, until Sherena usually gave in, just to get some peace.

Betsey wandered out into the back yard.

"Betsey, let's make a bow and some arrows. We could have an archery contest," said Desmond.

"No, thank you," Betsey sighed.

Desmond stared at her in disbelief.

Betsey had been asking him to show her how to make a bow and arrow from tree branches for the last month. And now, he'd offered to show her and she'd turned him down flat. Desmond watched as Betsey wandered back into the house.

Later that afternoon, Sherena whispered to Desmond, "Is Betsey back to normal yet?"

"No. And I offered to make a bow and arrow with her," said Desmond.

"I offered her a ride on my bike and she said no," said Sherena.

"This is serious," said Desmond.

And off they went to find Mam.

"Mam, we're worried about Betsey," said Sherena.

Just at that moment, the front door opened.

"We're here!" called out May's mam.

Mam, Sherena and Desmond went out into the sitting-room. May and her mam were standing there. May and Betsey stood facing each other but neither of them said a word.

"Betsey, say hello to May then," said Mam.

Betsey didn't say a word.

"May, say hello to your friend Betsey," said May's mam.

May turned her head away.

"It was the same thing last night," said May's mam. "May moped around the house and she hardly touched her dinner, but she wouldn't tell me what she and Betsey had argued about."

"All right then," Betsey's mam said firmly. "Betsey sit here. May, you sit down next to her."

Betsey sat down on the sofa and May sat down next to her, although they were careful not to touch each other.

"Right then, you two," said Mam.

"You're going to have an insult contest."

"An insult contest?" said Betsey, surprised.

"What's that?" asked May.

"Both of you will take it in turns to insult each other. The rest of us are going to sit opposite you and watch and listen. At the end of it we'll judge which one of you has come up with the best insult."

"But . . ."

"Oh, but . . ."

"No buts," said Mam, interrupting both May and Betsey. "Who wants to go first?"

May and Betsey frowned at each other.

"Okay, then," said Mam. "As you're the guest, May, you can go first. Think of an insult for Betsey."

May looked at Betsey, before looking down at her hands in her lap. She muttered something under her breath.

"We didn't quite catch that, May" said Mam. "Please say it again."

"I said that Betsey is a cabbage head," said May, very loudly this time.

"A cabbage head? Well, your head is shaped just like a dog biscuit and your ears are tiny like raisins!" said Betsey annoyed.

"So my head's like a dog biscuit, is it? Well, you're a . . . a . . . slimy snake . . ." began May.

"Ah! Can't allow that one," Mam interrupted. "Snakes aren't slimy. Their skin is quite dry."

Mam turned to May's mam and Sherena and Desmond. "Do you all agree?" she asked.

They all nodded.

"May, you'll have to come up with another insult," said Mam.

"Betsey is a toad face . . ." said May.

"You're a smelly sock . . ." said Betsey.

"You're a stinky sock . . ."

"You're more stinky than me . . ."

"No, I'm not . . ."

"Yes, you are . . ."

"You're a tissue that someone's blown their nose into lots and lots of times . . ." said May.

"You're the inside of Desmond's sweaty, smelly sports bag when he's been playing cricket," said Betsey.

Something very strange was happening. May's lips quivered and Betsey's lips twitched with each new insult that they flung at each other.

"Well, you're a . . . a . . ." May began.

"And you're a . . . you're a . . ." Betsey started.

But neither of them finished their insults. They both began to giggle, then to chuckle, then to roar with laughter. Which was just as well, because Betsey's mam and May's mam and Sherena and Desmond were all laughing so hard that they wouldn't have heard the next lot of insults anyway.

"I'm sorry, Betsey," smiled May.

"I'm sorry too," Betsey smiled back.

"So are you two friends again?" asked Mam.

Betsey and May nodded their heads.

"Glad to hear it," said May's mam. "What did you argue about in the first place?"

Betsey and May looked at each other, surprised.

"I can't remember," said Betsey.

"Neither can I!" said May.

"Never mind," said Betsey. "Let's go and play down by the beach."

"You bet!" said May.

Betsey and May bounced off the sofa and ran for the front door.

"Before you disappear, Betsey," said Desmond, calling after his sister, "I just want to say one thing."

"What's that?" asked Betsey.

"The inside of my sports bag is not sweaty and smelly!" said Desmond.

"Desmond, go and stick your nose in it and then say that," said Mam. "Betsey described your sports bag perfectly!"

Betsey and the Monster
Hamburger

"When we get there, I'm going to have a chicken burger," said Desmond.

"I'm going to have a veggie burger," said Sherena.

"I'm going to have a hamburger," said Betsey. "A big hamburger. The BIGGEST hamburger they've got. A MONSTER hamburger!"

The whole family was going to the local burger bar. For once, neither

Mam nor Gran'ma Liz had felt like cooking, so they were all going to eat out. It was a lovely evening. The air was warm and a gentle breeze was blowing.

"I'm going to have a strawberry milkshake," said Sherena.

"I think I'll have a vanilla one," said Desmond.

"I'm going to have two chocolate milkshakes," said Betsey, skipping down the road.

"Betsey, don't be such a pig," said Desmond.

"You'll never finish two milkshakes. It takes me ages just to finish one and my stomach is a lot bigger than yours," said Sherena.

"I'm going to have two - and you can't stop me," said Betsey.

"Betsey Biggalow, you will have one milkshake and like it," Mam

41

called out.

"But Mam, I'm really hungry," said Betsey.

"One, Betsey," said Mam firmly. "You'll have one milkshake or none at all."

"Botheration!" Betsey muttered under her breath. "I bet if it was Sherena or Desmond, they could have two if they wanted."

"Pardon, Betsey?" said Gran'ma Liz.

"Nothing, Gran'ma," Betsey replied.

Once they reached the burger bar, Mam asked each of them what they wanted. When it was Betsey's turn, Betsey said, "I want a MONSTER hamburger and two chocolate milkshakes and a large portion of French fries."

"Betsey, you'll have a small portion

of French fries and *one* chocolate milkshake." said Mam.

"But I'm starving."

"Betsey, your trouble is your eyes are bigger than your stomach. I'm

not going to buy all that food for you to leave most of it," said Mam.

"Can't I at least have the MONSTER hamburger?" sniffed Betsey.

"You'll never finish it," said Mam.

"I will. I promise," said Betsey. "*Please*."

"No, Betsey, you can't . . ." Mam began.

"Please, Mam. I will eat it. I'm starving hungry," said Betsey.

Mam frowned down at Betsey.

"All right then, Betsey," Mam said at last. "I'll buy you a MONSTER hamburger and you'd better eat it. I don't want to see any left."

"You won't," Betsey beamed.

"Hhmm!" Was all Gran'ma Liz said.

Desmond and Mam went up to the counter to order whilst Gran'ma Liz, Sherena and Betsey found a table. It didn't take long for Mam and Desmond to join them, each carrying a tray filled with food.

Betsey licked her lips. Her very

first MONSTER hamburger! She was going to enjoy this!

Mam put Betsey's MONSTER hamburger in front of her.

"There you are, Betsey," said Mam.

"Thanks, Mam," Betsey grinned.

"Eating that will soon wipe the grin off your face, Elizabeth Ruby Biggalow," said Gran'ma Liz.

"Botheration!" said Betsey. "Gran'ma, I will finish this hamburger. Just watch."

"I intend to," said Gran'ma Liz.

And with that they all started to eat.

Betsey picked up her hamburger with both hands. She looked at it from above, she looked at it from below, she checked each side of it. It was HUGE! In fact it was so big, she hardly knew where to begin.

"Anything wrong, Betsey?" asked

Mam.

"No, Mam," Betsey replied.

Then she opened her eyes W-I-D-E and opened her mouth W-I-D-E-R and bit into her hamburger. Tomato ketchup squirted out one side of the hamburger and hit Desmond - PLOOPPP! - on the nose. A dollop of mustard flew out of the other side of the hamburger and hit Sherena - SPLATTT! - on the forehead.

"Betsey, look what you've done. I

look like I've got a nose bleed," said
Desmond, annoyed.

"Betsey, watch what you're doing,"
said Sherena, wiping the mustard off
her face.

"Well done, Betsey," laughed
Mam. "You managed to get two
people with just one bite."

Betsey chewed and chewed away at
the piece of hamburger she had
managed to bite off. Then she had
some French fries and washed it all

down with some chocolate milkshake. It was all double delicious!
Betsey took another bite and
another, then another.

The only trouble was, she was
beginning to feel full and she hadn't
even eaten half of the burger yet.
Betsey chewed more and more
slowly, as she became more and
more full.

"What's the matter, Betsey? Is that
hamburger too much for you?"
asked Gran'ma Liz.

"Oh no, Gran'ma," Betsey replied
quickly. "I'm just eating it slowly so
that I can remember what every
mouthful tastes like."

Gran'ma Liz and Mam exchanged
a look.

"Hhmm!" Was all Gran'ma said.

What am I going to do? thought
Betsey as she chewed on yet another

mouthful. She was stuffed! If she had just one more bite, she would pop like a balloon. But if she stopped now, everyone would say, 'We told you so!'

Then Betsey had an idea. She arranged the paper napkin on her lap to cover her skirt. She broke off a bit of her burger. Then she pretended to put the piece of burger into her mouth but she didn't really . . . Whilst she was pretending to chew, Betsey waited until no one was looking and dropped the little bit of burger from her hand into her napkin. As soon as the coast was clear, Betsey did the same thing again. She broke off a piece and pretended to eat it, but instead dropped it into her napkin. Ten pieces later, there was no more hamburger left in her hands - but lots of pieces of hamburger sat on the napkin in her lap. Betsey folded up the napkin until none of the hamburger could be seen.

Betsey picked up her chocolate milkshake and took a long drink. Pretending to eat hamburger was very thirsty work!

"Well done, Betsey!" Mam said surprised. "I must admit, I didn't think you could do it."

"I told you I was hungry," said Betsey.

"Your appetite has doubled overnight - and so has your stomach," said Gran'ma Liz.

"Okay everyone, pass over your napkins and empty wrappers and cups and I'll put them all on this tray," said Mam.

Oh no! thought Betsey. She couldn't hand over her napkin to

Mam. Her mam would feel the napkin and immediately guess what was in it. That's when Betsey had another idea.

She deliberately dropped her knife on the floor.

"I'll just pick that up," said Betsey, and she scooted under the table.

Quick as a jack-rabbit, Betsey opened up Sherena's handbag and put in the napkin filled with all the pieces of hamburger. Then she got the knife and sat up again, putting the knife on one of the trays.

"Come on then, everyone. Let's go home," said Mam. And they all stood up.

On the way home Sherena said, "Well done, Betsey. I didn't think you'd finish that hamburger. I've never been able to finish one of those in my life."

Betsey said nothing. What could she say? And there was just one thing on her mind. How was she going to get the napkin filled with hamburger out of Sherena's bag without anyone finding out.

Botheration! thought Betsey. Double and triple botheration!

"Sherena, do you want me to carry your handbag?" Betsey asked hopefully.

"What on earth for?" asked

Sherena.

"No reason."

"No, thank you," said Sherena.

Just at that moment, Betsey felt the back of her neck go all tingly and hot. She turned around and there was Gran'ma Liz standing right behind her. And Gran'ma Liz had that look in her eyes. The look that said, 'Betsey, you're up to something. I don't know what it is, but we both know I'm going to find out!'

And it didn't take her long to find out either! Betsey followed Sherena into the house, hoping for a chance to take her napkin out of Sherena's handbag. But no sooner had they taken just a couple of steps into the house than Prince, the Alsatian dog, came bounding up to Sherena and started sniffing at her handbag.

"Prince, what are you doing?" frowned Sherena.

Prince snatched the handbag and raced off around the sitting-room with it. Sherena chased after him, followed by Betsey and Desmond.

"What's the matter with that dog?" asked Mam.

"I think I know," said Gran'ma Liz. "Prince, sit! Sit!"

Immediately Prince did as he was told.

"Sherena, bring me your handbag," said Gran'ma Liz.

Sherena handed over her bag to Gran'ma.

"Now then, Betsey," said Gran'ma Liz. "Is there anything you want to say before I open this handbag?"

"Just that I'm sorry and I won't do it again," Betsey sniffed.

"Hhmm!" said Gran'ma Liz. And she opened the handbag.

"What's going on?" asked Sherena, puzzled.

Gran'ma Liz looked at Betsey. Betsey looked up at Gran'ma Liz. Gran'ma Liz took the napkin out of

Sherena's handbag and put it in her cardigan pocket.

"Nothing's going on," said Gran'ma Liz at last. "Isn't that right, Betsey?"

"That's right, Gran'ma," said Betsey, in a tiny voice.

Betsey couldn't believe it. Gran'ma Liz wasn't going to tell anyone what she'd done!

"Betsey, the next time we go to the burger bar, what are you going to have?" asked Gran'ma Liz.

"One milkshake and a small portion of fries," Betsey replied.

"No MONSTER hamburger?" asked Sherena.

"I don't care if I never see another hamburger again as long as I live," said Betsey.

And she meant it!

A Selected List of Fiction from Mammoth

While every effort is made to keep prices low, it is sometimes necessary to increase prices at short notice. Mandarin Paperbacks reserves the right to show new retail prices on covers which may differ from those previously advertised in the text or elsewhere.

The prices shown below were correct at the time of going to press.

☐	7497 1421 2	**Betsey Biggalow is Here!**	Malorie Blackman	£2.99
☐	7497 0366 0	**Dilly the Dinosaur**	Tony Bradman	£2.99
☐	7497 0137 4	**Flat Stanley**	Jeff Brown	£2.99
☐	7497 0983 9	**The Real Tilly Beany**	Annie Dalton	£2.99
☐	7497 0592 2	**The Peacock Garden**	Anita Desai	£2.99
☐	7497 0054 8	**My Naughty Little Sister**	Dorothy Edwards	£2.99
☐	7497 0723 2	**The Little Prince (colour ed.)**	A. Saint-Exupery	£3.99
☐	7497 0305 9	**Bill's New Frock**	Anne Fine	£2.99
☐	7497 1718 1	**My Grandmother's Stories**	Adèle Geras	£2.99
☐	7497 0041 6	**The Quiet Pirate**	Andrew Matthews	£2.99
☐	7497 1930 3	**The Jessame Stories**	Julia Jarman	£2.99
☐	7497 0420 9	**I Don't Want To!**	Bel Mooney	£2.99
☐	7497 1496 4	**Miss Bianca in the Orient**	Margery Sharp	£2.99
☐	7497 0048 3	**Friends and Brothers**	Dick King Smith	£2.99
☐	7497 0795 X	**Owl Who Was Afraid of the Dark**	Jill Tomlinson	£2.99
☐	7497 0915 4	**Little Red Fox Stories**	Alison Uttley	£2.99

All these books are available at your bookshop or newsagent, or can be ordered direct from the address below. Just tick the titles you want and fill in the form below.

Cash Sales Department, PO Box 5, Rushden, Northants NN10 6YX.
Fax: 01933 414047 : Phone: 01933 414000.

Please send cheque, payable to 'Reed Book Services Ltd.', or postal order for purchase price quoted and allow the following for postage and packing:

£1.00 for the first book, 50p for the second; **FREE POSTAGE AND PACKING FOR THREE BOOKS OR MORE PER ORDER.**

NAME (Block letters) ....

ADDRESS ....

....

☐ I enclose my remittance for ....

☐ I wish to pay by Access/Visa Card Number

Expiry Date

Signature ....

Please quote our reference: MAND